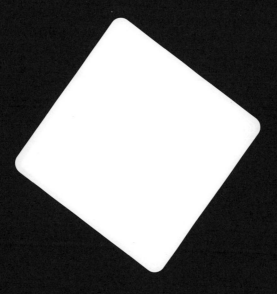

Parker Bell

and the SCIENCE of

FRIENDSHIP

Parker Bell and the SCIENCE of FRIENDSHIP

written by **CYNTHIA PLATT**

illustrated by **REA ZHAI**

CLARION BOOKS

HOUGHTON MIFFLIN HARCOURT

BOSTON   NEW YORK

Clarion Books
3 Park Avenue
New York, New York 10016

Clarion Books is an imprint of Houghton Mifflin Harcourt Publishing
Company.

hmhbooks.com

The text was set in Stempel Garamond LT.

Library of Congress Cataloging-in-Publication Data
Names: Platt, Cynthia, author. | Zhai, Rea, illustrator.
Title: Parker Bell and the science of friendship / Cynthia Platt ;
illustrations by Rea Zhai.
Description: Boston ; New York : Clarion Books,
Houghton Mifflin Harcourt,
[2019] | Summary: "Parker really wants to win the school Science
Triathlon—but first she'll have to figure out how to keep her BFF from
being stolen" — Provided by publisher.
Identifiers: LCCN 2018035176 | ISBN 9781328973474 (hardback)
Subjects: | CYAC: Best friends — Fiction. | Friendship — Fiction. |
Science — Competitions — Fiction. | Schools — Fiction. |
Robots — Fiction. | BISAC: JUVENILE FICTION / Social Issues /
Friendship. | JUVENILE FICTION /
Science & Technology. | JUVENILE FICTION / Girls & Women.
Classification: LCC PZ7.P7124 Par 2019 | DDC [Fic] — dc23
LC record available at https://lccn.loc.gov/2018035176

Printed in the United States of America
DOC 10 9 8 7 6 5 4 3 2 1
4500754853

To John,
who liked to build contraptions,
and to Barbara,
who had to endure them with me.
—C.P.

Contents

Chapter 1

The Fashion Experiment

Parker Bell loved science. One day, she hoped to be a world-famous scientist, making important discoveries and engineering robots to help people do amazing and exciting things. But first, she had to finish going to Eleanor Roosevelt Elementary School.

And before she did that, she had to get dressed for what was going to be one of the best, most important days of science at school ever.

The getting dressed part was proving difficult.

"Parker, just pick out some clothes. It doesn't matter which ones!" her mom called. "You're going to be late."

"I'll be right there!" Parker yelled back.

Still in her pajamas, Parker stood in front of her closet and tried to figure out what to wear so she

would look strong and smart and scientific. After trying on (and taking back off again) three different outfits, though, she knew she needed a plan.

But where to start? If Parker could use a scientific method of inquiry for her experiments, maybe she could use that to get dressed, too. She figured it was worth a try.

INITIAL QUESTION: What is the perfect outfit to wear for today's Big Science Announcement?

BRAINSTORM SOLUTIONS: Dressing like a fierce animal might show everyone how fierce my interest in science is.

GATHER DATA: In my closet, I have dresses in zebra and leopard patterns, and a black-and-white one that looks like an orca. Orcas are definitely the smartest of those three animals.

USE DATA TO MAKE A PREDICTION: So if I dress like an orca, then my classmates and Ms. Garcia will see how smart and scientific I am. Everyone will notice this and know how excited I am about science and the announcement today!

Okay, so this wasn't strictly scientific. But at least Parker could get the reactions of her parents and friends to have some evidence to communicate about her experiment afterward. Treating it as an experiment also definitely helped her pick out the right clothes for the day: her black-and-white dress and black boots with tassels on the back. To top off her outfit, she put on a satin headband with tiny orcas embroidered all over it. Because today she needed to be strong and smart, just like an orca.

When Parker stopped to gaze at herself in the mirror, she knew she had a great look going.

Then she saw her favorite scientists staring at her from the posters over her bed. Jane Goodall had a look of gentle disappointment on her face. The same one Parker's mother had worn when Parker took apart the toaster in her Mad Science Lab last summer to see how it worked. It had frustrated Parker *and* her mother when Parker discovered toasters are easier to take apart than put back together.

"I know you don't dress up," Parker told Poster

Jane. "But just because you live with chimpanzees doesn't mean that I do!"

This didn't seem to change Jane's mind in any way, so Parker turned to her other favorite scientist. "You get it, Mae," she said. "I know you do."

Mae Jemison smiled down at Parker from her poster, looking pretty amazing herself in her orange astronaut flight suit. Parker could see that Mae understood.

"And you do too, don't you, Algebra?" Parker knelt by her guinea pig's cage to scratch the little piggy behind his ears, making him squeak happily. She flicked the lever on the robotic guinea pig feeder she'd built over the course of last summer. She'd attached some of the toaster parts to cogs from her Mad Science Lab. It turned out that the same device that lifted bread out of the toaster was also great for lifting a box of rodent pellets, which then poured through a funnel into Algebra's bowl. Parker had thought the robotic feeder was a great way to recycle and reuse, but her mom hadn't been too thrilled about having to buy a new toaster.

And now her mom was calling from down the hall. "PARKER! You're going to miss the bus!"

"Oops — coming!" Parker called back. She turned to Algebra. "I'll catch your sweet furry face later."

She could hear Algebra squeaking loudly as she ran to the kitchen. She paused in the kitchen doorway, waiting for her mom to look up and notice her orca outfit. This was the first test of her fashion experiment, and Parker couldn't wait to see what would happen!

But her mother looked at her as if this were any other day and any other outfit. "Dad brought these up from the bakery," her mom said, pointing to two ginormous blueberry muffins. "One for you and one for Cassie. You're going to have to eat on the bus, though, because you're so late."

Parker stayed in the doorway for another second, hoping her mother would say something else.

Something maybe about her scientifically chosen outfit.

"What are you waiting for?" her mom said, totally skipping over the important stuff. "The bus is coming!"

Parker's first test of her prediction was a bust. Her mom totally didn't notice any correlation between Parker's clothes and the Big Science Announcement at school. With a sigh, Parker scooped up the muffins and opened the back door, yelling down to the bakery on the first floor, "Thanks, Dad!" before running downstairs to catch the bus.

"Have a good day!" her mom called behind her. Parker still thought she was the most amazing mom ever, even if she didn't test well with Parker's scientifically chosen fashion. Or understand Parker's sense of style in general. Or appreciate her interest in taking apart small appliances in the name of science.

Besides, Parker was very sure her best friend, Cassie Malouf, would understand her outfit and prove that it was scientifically the best she could have worn.

o o o

When Parker got on the bus, though, she didn't see Cassie in their seat, the sixth row on the left. Cassie was *always* in their seat.

Instead, Theo Zachary was sitting there, being his extra-tall, big-eared self. Parker was not a big fan of Theo. He had been her science partner once in second grade. He didn't talk to her at all during the entire class. And he spilled so much water during their sink-or-float experiment that *nothing* could sink or float in the end. They got a one out of four on that assignment.

Parker Bell had never gotten a one out of four in science before that. Ever. It hadn't been a good feeling.

Now Theo was on her school bus. Sitting in her seat. Where Cassie should be sitting.

"Parker!" Cassie called. She was sitting in the ninth row on the right, in a seat that definitely wasn't theirs.

Parker and Cassie had been best friends since the first day of kindergarten. They had read a story in class about a girl and her baby sister, and Parker had gotten down in the dumps on the bus ride home. No matter how much she wanted one, there was no baby sister happening in her family. "And there isn't going to be one, honey," her mom would remind her whenever Parker brought it up.

"Having a baby sister isn't all that," Cassie had reassured her. "Mine stinks."

At first Parker had thought Cassie meant she didn't like having a baby sister.

"No, I mean she smells bad," Cassie had told her. "Her diapers are the worst of the worst."

Five-year-old Parker wasn't convinced. "Even if she's smelly, she's still yours," she'd replied. "I'm all by myself."

With a shrug, Cassie had said, "It's much better to have a best friend than a baby sister."

That had only made Parker feel worse. Not only did she not have a baby sister, she wasn't all that sure she had a best friend. Or any friends. She mentioned this to Cassie.

"You have me," Cassie told her. "I'll be your best friend."

They had been besties ever since.

o   o   o

Now Parker rushed past Theo on the bus to find her BFF. "Why's he on our bus?" Parker asked as she handed Cassie a muffin. "And in our seat?"

"I don't know," Cassie mumbled through a mouthful of muffin. "I should have asked when we were talking just now."

"You were talking to Theo Zachary?" Parker asked. "Why?"

"He's in the new Coders' Club with me," Cassie told her. "We're going to make a video game together. He's nice."

A bad feeling started to brew in Parker's stomach, as if she'd mixed vinegar and baking soda together inside her and made a fizzy volcanic eruption.

Parker wasn't in the Coders' Club for one simple reason: all they ever seemed to do was make online games, and she didn't like to play them, let alone code them. But Cassie loved playing these games and also trying to make them herself. While Parker knew that Cassie had joined the Coders' Club, she hadn't known that her best friend was now gamer friends with Theo. Parker hadn't known Cassie was friends with *anyone* other than her.

Cassie didn't seem to notice that Parker had gone quiet. Now that Parker was thinking about it, Cassie hadn't noticed her outfit, either. Parker's scientific fashion experiment had totally failed. No one knew she was a strong and smart orca ready for amazing science announcements.

"Hey," Cassie said, nudging Parker's shoulder. Her best friend opened *The Big Book of Ginormous Facts*. Parker had given it to Cassie for her birthday. Cassie couldn't put it down.

"'Orcas are some of the fiercest hunters in nature. *How fierce are they?*'" Cassie read. "'Sometimes they play with their food, tossing seals high in the air before eating them. Just to show them who's boss!'"

"That is fierce," Parker agreed.

She was wondering whether or not to tell her BFF about her failed experiment when Cassie said, "And your orca outfit is fierce too."

At last Parker had some good results! She was so happy she'd worn black and white to look like an orca today. She was extra-super happy she had the kind of best friend who noticed things like that.

Sure, her test results were incomplete, but it wasn't a real scientific inquiry after all. Her mother was a PE teacher who always dressed like she was in PE class (even on Saturdays!), so she probably would never notice good fashion, scientifically chosen or otherwise. Cassie, on the other hand, noticed every tiny detail about everything.

It was one of the reasons Parker loved her so much. And it was almost enough to make Parker forget that Cassie was becoming friends with Theo Zachary.

Almost, but not quite.

Chapter 2

The Big Science Announcement

Waiting was not one of Parker Bell's talents. She was good at doing lots of things, like being fashionable and taking care of guinea pigs. She was also good at watching Morph-Bots shows and reading Morph-Bots comic books. And she was extra-super good at science and building robots.

But waiting . . . well, that was a struggle. By the time she got through morning meeting, language arts, social studies, and PE, she was losing patience. Even art took too long. All Parker wanted was to hear the Big Science Announcement. She didn't think it was so much to ask, really. How could Ms. Garcia tell them that there'd be a big announcement on Friday and then make them wait all day to hear it?

Here it was, though, 2:15 in the afternoon and still nothing. Soon it would be time to pack up and go home. And then there would be two whole days of weekend before she could come back to school.

Parker wasn't just losing her patience. She was beginning to lose her cool. What she needed was a distraction.

The class rules usually helped. Her class had come up with them together on the first day of school. Parker found it calming to read them over and over again, especially rules like "Be Kind with Your Words & Actions" and "Respect Others' Thoughts & Feelings." She also liked "Always Tell the Truth," as any good scientist would always be truthful about her findings.

There was only one rule that Parker didn't agree with: "Work Carefully, Quietly, and Neatly." She was 100 percent behind *carefully* and *neatly*. But *quietly* was not for her. Unfortunately, only she and Aidan, Braidan, and Jaidan, the annoying Dempsey Triplets, hadn't voted for that rule, so it passed.

Just thinking about being on the same side as the Dempsey Triplets got Parker peeved.

So she did the one thing that *always* helped her find her cool again at school: she started observing Snodgrass, the class lizard. He was a brown gecko and he ate live crickets. He was slowly stalking a cricket in his tank right now. Soon he would open his wide lizard mouth and that cricket would be a goner.

Parker was waiting for her turn to feed Snodgrass. She had a secret plan to eat one of the crickets herself. Just to see what would happen, for scientific purposes. What would it taste like? Would she be able to feel its legs moving as she swallowed it?

Unfortunately, Parker had no way to know yet because it wouldn't be her turn to feed Snodgrass for weeks and weeks. Ms. Garcia had decided to start at the back of the alphabet for taking turns. She said it was to be fair.

Parker thought it stunk. Because she, Parker Bell, was at the very beginning of the alphabet. Theo Zachary, on the other hand, was at the very end. Which meant he had already gotten to feed Snodgrass. And had totally blown his chance to eat a cricket.

Ms. Garcia had listened closely when Parker explained that this was too long to wait. (She'd left out the part about eating a cricket for science.) Then Ms. Garcia laid the worst of the worst teacher lines down on her.

"You get what you get, and you don't get upset, Parker!"

If there was one thing Parker hated, it was getting what she got. Well, also chickens. Chickens creeped her out. And she wasn't a big fan of cauliflower. Plus, the thought of Cassie becoming friends with Theo didn't make Parker too happy either.

There were actually a lot of things that got her peeved when she stopped to think about it. But getting what she got was definitely top ten.

"Pay attention," Cassie whispered to Parker. "You're going to miss everything!"

Suddenly, Snodgrass and his crickets weren't half

as interesting as they had been. It was finally time for the Big Science Announcement!

"Starting next week, we're going to have a new school competition," Ms. Garcia told them as she handed out large packets of papers. "It's a Science Triathlon, with three events over the course of three weeks." Turned out that meant a Science Bee (like a spelling bee but with science questions) and an Egg Drop after school, and then Animal Adaptation Presentations at a schoolwide assembly. You'd compete against kids in your class, and from other classes too, and get extra credit. Plus, there were going to be gold, silver, and bronze medals for the winners.

Ms. Garcia smiled at the class. "Anyone who's interested will have to compete in teams," she continued. "And I have a packet of information for each of you to bring home and share with your parents."

Parker sat up straight in her chair. This was the best news ever. She would be on a team with Cassie! Between Cassie's coding and trivia know-how and

Parker's engineering skills, they'd get extra credit *and* win a science award. It would be Parker's first step in becoming a world-famous scientist just like Jane Goodall and Mae Jemison!

Not everyone was taking the announcement as seriously as Parker, though. She glanced over at Aidan and Jaidan and Braidan Dempsey and sighed. They were taking turns kicking their fellow triplets under their desks instead of listening. They were not acting like they were interested in extra credit or scientific gold medals. They probably weren't going to participate in the Science Triathlon.

As Ms. Garcia dismissed class, Aidan stopped kicking his brothers and walked over to Parker.

"Are you doing the Triathlon?" he asked her.

"Of course!" she replied as she packed up her backpack.

"Who are you going to team up with?" Aidan asked her.

Parker couldn't believe she and Aidan were

talking about the Science Triathlon. They never talked about anything, let alone school stuff.

"I'm teaming with Cassie," Parker told him, because of course she was. She always did. "Why?"

"No reason," Aidan said. Without another word, he turned to join his brothers, grabbing Jaidan in a headlock and popping his backpack over his shoulder. She watched him as he left the classroom with his fellow triplets. Parker wondered if he might have been looking for a partner for the Science Triathlon, but then she realized what a crazy idea that was. The Dempsey Triplets were never serious about anything, let alone totally voluntary science projects.

Besides, she and Cassie were a dynamic duo. A team of two, now and always. They didn't need Aidan or anyone else to help them do science.

At least, Parker had thought that was the case. Then Cassie came over, dragging her backpack and Theo Zachary behind her.

"Good news!" Cassie told Parker. "Theo wants to

do the Science Triathlon too, so I told him he could be on our team." Her best friend in the whole world smiled at Theo, and Parker suddenly felt like she'd eaten a whole box of Snodgrass's crickets at once and they were dancing all the way down to her stomach.

Cassie hadn't even checked with her before asking Theo to be on their team. Parker couldn't believe this was happening.

Sure, she still got to be on a team with Cassie. But now she had to work with Theo, too. The dynamic, scientific duo was going to be a not-so-dynamic, not-so-scientific trio.

Being an award-winning scientist like Jane and Mae seemed about as likely to happen as Parker's bus traveling at light speed on the way to school.

Chapter 3

Coders' Club Science

As soon as the bell rang, everyone filed out of the classroom. Parker sighed and slung her Morph-Bots backpack over her shoulders. She wanted to be excited to work with someone new, but she just wasn't. Parker and Cassie were complementary angles, just like they'd learned in math. Cassie was a whiz at remembering stuff and Parker hated memorization. Cassie liked to engineer things on the computer and Parker liked to engineer things in real life. Cassie wore skinny jeans and plaid shirts, while Parker always wore dresses. Cassie was always on time and Parker was always late.

They were two angles that fit together perfectly.

Theo would just get in the way.

When Parker climbed onto the bus, Theo was in her and Cassie's seat again. This time, Cassie was sitting in front of him, leafing through her Science Triathlon packet. As soon as Parker plunked down in the fifth seat on the left, Cassie knelt on the bus seat so she could talk to Parker and Theo at the same time. Cassie clearly didn't have the same doubts about this whole situation that Parker had.

"It says here that all the Science Bee questions will be about weather and climate," she told them. "Do you guys want to come over to my house tomorrow to start studying for it?"

"Yes!" Parker said. Going to Cassie's house was almost as good as being at home, especially when her little sister, Mara, was there. Plus, Cassie's mom was a mathematician, and Parker loved talking numbers with her. The only downside was the food. Unless Cassie's jaddah had come over recently to fill the fridge with her delicious cooking, Cassie's parents usually got take-out. Disappointingly, Cassie's

grandmother didn't visit that often, despite Parker's obsession with her biryani. But that wasn't Cassie's fault. Not everyone's parents could cook the way Parker's dad could.

Besides, Cassie had all the fact books in the world in her room. It might not have been a Mad Science Lab, but there was a *lot* of good information, which was just what they needed to start preparing for the Science Bee.

"Theo, can you let your mom know that you need to go to Cassie's tomorrow?" Parker said.

Theo turned the brightest color of red Parker had ever seen anyone turn.

"Theo?" Cassie said in a much quieter voice than Parker had used. "Can you come?"

Theo didn't say a word. He just nodded quickly and turned to look out the window.

Parker took a deep breath. This was going to be bad. Really bad.

o   o   o

Things didn't get better when Parker got to Cassie's house the next day. Cassie's mom let her in. "I think I might celebrate Pi Day early this year," she said. "Maybe one of your dad's apple pies will keep my students awake!"

"How could anyone fall asleep in your calculus class?" Parker asked.

"Not everyone likes math as much as you do," Cassie's mom replied. "When you're in college, maybe you can take one of my courses."

That sounded like heaven to Parker. The only thing that could be better right now was some biryani, but there were no mouthwatering spicy smells coming from the kitchen. Which was too bad, because Parker could really go for some of Cassie's jaddah's yummy chicken and rice.

When Parker went to Cassie's room to help her BFF pick out the right trivia books for them to study, she discovered Theo was already there. He had a laptop open on his knees, and Cassie's cat, Cleopatra, was curled up next to him.

"Thanks for bringing my book back!" Cassie said, as Parker handed her BFF *Lightning and Thunder and Hail — Oh My!* Of course, Parker had borrowed it only because Cassie had kept telling her that she'd love it, even though it wasn't really Parker's thing. But Parker figured she would actually love it now that they needed it for the Science Bee.

"The more books to study with, the better," Parker said, as she grabbed another with 10,001 facts about the weather, as well as *The Weather: Just the Facts!* and another about hurricanes off Cassie's shelf. Parker sat down under Cassie's cartoon poster of Mario and the guy who created him, Shigeru Miyamoto.

"These books are amazing!" Parker said. She and Cassie locked knuckles and made their fingers dance. "We are going to slay the Science Bee!"

"We are," Cassie agreed. "But that's not all we have to help us study!"

Since Parker had arrived at Cassie's house, all Theo had done was look at his computer screen and pet the cat. He hadn't said a single word other than "Hi" the whole time, not even to Cleopatra.

Now he was grinning at Cassie, who grinned right back at him.

"What do you mean?" Parker asked, feeling suddenly left out.

"I'd already started to make an online trivia game in Coders' Club, but I fixed it up to help us study!" Cassie said, opening her own laptop. "We answer science questions, and for each one we get right, we get a prize in the game."

"But don't you know all the answers if you made the game?" Parker asked. "That will only help me and Theo, not you."

"My mom put all the questions in so I wouldn't see the answers," Cassie said. Then she smiled at Theo. "And Theo came over early to help me set up the game prizes," she said. "He's in the Coders' Club too, remember? So now we can all play a game *and* get ready for the Science Bee!"

Parker was kerflummoxed. She knew Theo had

gotten to Cassie's house before her, but she hadn't realized that he'd gotten there early enough to help code a game.

Cassie was looking at her expectantly, so Parker knew she had to say something. "That's an awesome idea," Parker told them. "Especially the prizes."

"Great! Then let's start playing!"

Cassie put her computer on Parker's lap, then read the first trivia question out loud: "What do you call a hurricane in the Southern Hemisphere?"

"T-Y-P-H-O-O-N?" Parker typed in the answer as she spoke.

"No, a cyclone!" Cassie said. Parker was bummed she didn't get a prize for her first question, but it only made her want to get the next one right even more.

"What do you call precipitation that forms as a liquid but freezes on the way down?" Parker read aloud from the laptop.

S-L-E-E-T, she typed. Suddenly, the screen went bright yellow and the head of her most favorite Morph-Bot character appeared on the screen.

"Ultra-Megabot!" Parker exclaimed. "This trivia game is amazing!"

"I knew you'd like it," Cassie said. "Every time you get a question right, you build another part of Ultra-Megabot."

Parker smiled, even though she knew you couldn't build robots from the head down. You had to start with an internal engine, of course. She was about to tell Cassie that, but then decided it was more important to study for the Science Bee together. Plus, Cassie had picked rewards that were something Parker loved so much. She didn't want her friend to think she didn't like the game.

"Theo likes Morph-Bots too," Cassie told her. "So I thought this would be fun for both of you!"

Or Cassie had made the game so Theo would love the prizes too. It was nice of Cassie to think of Theo, of course. But Parker had been much happier with the idea of Cassie thinking only about her.

Parker knew she should say something polite in response to this news, but she didn't want to. She looked down at the laptop to avoid having to reply. The next question had her stumped, though. "Does anyone know what type of cloud hail forms in?"

Cassie shrugged. Her mom had put in some really hard questions!

Then a very quiet voice came from the general direction of the cat. It wasn't Cleopatra talking, though. It was Theo. Somehow it might have been less shocking if the cat *had* answered.

"Cumulonimbus," he almost whispered. It looked like he was telling the answer to the cat.

It was so surprising to hear Theo talk that Parker didn't know what to say.

Finally, she asked him how to spell it. As soon as she typed in the letters, Ultra-Megabot's neck and middle section appeared. *Still not how to build a robot,* Parker thought. But she pushed that thought aside and turned to consider Theo for a minute.

Parker still did not want to share Cassie with Theo. But maybe he wouldn't be such dead weight on their team after all.

Chapter 4

Molecules Have a Party

On the day of the Science Bee, Cassie looked fierce in her *I Know 10,001 Facts About Everything* T-shirt. Parker looked fierce in her red dress with the asymmetrical skirt.

After school, as the Science Bee was starting, Theo looked miserable.

His face was as red as Parker's dress and he kept looking down at the floor. Then he started biting his nails.

"We're doomed," Parker whispered to Cassie.

Her BFF shrugged. "It'll be okay," she said. "He's just nervous. Plus, I studied hard for this."

"Me too," Parker said. Even though she usually hated gaming and memorizing facts, she'd been using Cassie and Theo's game constantly to prep for the Science Bee.

She wanted to win science glory in the Triathlon! It wouldn't be like winning a Nobel Prize, but it would still take her one step closer to being like Jane and Mae.

Parker really wanted to be like Jane and Mae.

What's more, she wanted to beat the Dempsey Triplets, who'd surprised everyone by showing up after school for the Science Bee. Parker looked over at them. Braidan and Jaidan were making fart noises with their hands, but Aidan was reading a notebook instead of goofing off.

How the Dempsey Triplets thought they were going to win a Science Bee was a puzzle, but having them there made Parker start to feel nervous too.

She took a deep breath and held out her hand to Cassie. They locked knuckles and danced their fingers. Parker saw that Theo was watching. Never once, in the whole history of the handshake, had Parker or Cassie asked anyone else to do it.

Until that moment, when Parker's very best friend in the world held out her hand to Theo. They locked knuckles, but Theo didn't dance his fingers at all.

Parker wanted to be happy that Cassie had made a new friend. She really did.

But mostly she wasn't.

So, when Cassie nudged her, it took Parker a second to figure out that Cassie wanted her to do their handshake with Theo too. Parker took a deep breath and held her hand out to him so he could do the secret handshake with her.

She ended up bumping his hand and startling him. Theo's hand dropped to his side and he made a funny face. Grandma Bell always said if you made a face like that, it might stick. Parker knew scientifically that wasn't possible. But she still wished Theo wasn't making that face at her.

"Sorry," Parker muttered, dropping her own hand.

Each team had to sit together. Ms. Garcia had them move their desks into a circle, but Theo kept his desk a little ways apart from Parker's and Cassie's.

Whatever hope Parker had had for Theo as a teammate was gone. He didn't even want to sit with them. Or do the handshake with her. She and Cassie were perfect partners. Theo was just dead weight.

o o o

Fortunately, the first round of questions for the Science Bee was easy-peasy: Animals and Climate. At least, the questions were easy for Parker and Cassie. They made it to the next round without Theo's help.

Two of the six teams weren't so lucky.

That meant four teams were left for round two: All About the Water Cycle.

The first few questions weren't that hard if you'd studied. Which Parker and Cassie had. But so had the three girls on the team next to them. Parker recognized them from Mr. Tanner's class, though she didn't know their names. They gave the right answer without even hesitating.

Then it was the Dempsey Triplets' turn.

"Name five main forms of precipitation," Ms. Garcia asked.

While Braidan and Jaidan had stopped making fart noises, they definitely didn't look like they knew the answer.

"Rain, drizzle, snow, sleet, and hail," Aidan said.

"Correct!" Ms. Garcia said. The Dempsey Triplets high-fived.

Parker was kerflummoxed. Had Aidan really just answered that hard Science Bee question correctly?

Next, a team of three boys from Ms. Chang's class went down on a question about what happens to water when a teakettle boils. Parker wasn't sure whether they didn't know the answer or didn't know what a teakettle was. Either way, they were out. They looked so embarrassed that Parker felt bad for them.

That left just three teams for the start of the next

round: Parker and Cassie and Theo, the three girls from Mr. Tanner's class, and the Dempsey Triplets.

Parker and her crew aced their next question about how water molecules behave as a solid, liquid, and gas.

"When water freezes, the molecules clump together," Cassie said.

"And when they're liquid, they move around and bounce off each other," Parker added.

They looked at Theo to see if he was going to answer the part about gas molecules.

He bit his nails instead.

This made Parker mad because she knew he had the answer. He'd gotten it right in the trivia game when they had practiced at Cassie's house.

Still, he didn't say a word.

"And when water's a gas, the molecules move all over the place like they're having a party," Parker said.

"Good work!" Ms. Garcia said.

Then she asked the team of girls what kind of

clouds produce hail. It was the same question Theo had gotten right at Cassie's house! It seemed these girls didn't know the answer, though. They looked at one another and shrugged.

One of them finally guessed, "Cumulus?"

Ms. Garcia shook her head. "Sorry, girls," she said. Then she turned to the group. "Do either of the other teams know the answer?"

Parker nudged Theo, trying to get him to respond before the Dempseys figured out the answer. It was his big moment to shine, after all. But Theo didn't seem to want to shine. He got even redder and hunched his tall self down really low in his seat.

"Don't worry, I've got this," Cassie said to him with a smile. She called out, "Cumulonimbus!"

With a big grin, Ms. Garcia said, "That's correct!" before moving on to the next question.

"How has the amount of water on our planet changed over time?" she asked the Dempseys.

There was no way these boys had the answer to this one, Parker thought. But she was wrong.

"There's always been the same amount of water," Aidan said.

"Which means that the water we drink now used to be dinosaur pee!" Jaidan added.

Most of the other kids snickered, but Parker didn't. How did Aidan know that answer? Something weird was going on. He was always goofing off in class. Had he been secretly paying attention?

As she sat wondering, Parker's team got a question about ice turning directly into a gas, which Cassie answered correctly. Parker knew the process was sublimation, but she was too distracted to speak up.

Could the Dempsey Triplets actually win the Science Bee?

Ms. Garcia lobbed another question at the brothers. "What percent of the earth's water is freshwater?"

This was a hard one. The kind of question you had to have *really* studied for to get right. And it seemed like only one of the triplets had done any studying.

The Dempsey Triplets got in a huddle and mumbled until Aidan finally shook his head and said, "Twenty-five percent is freshwater?"

But that wasn't the right answer. Parker knew it wasn't. She'd answered this trivia question in the video game and won Ultra-Megabot's left leg with it.

The Dempsey Triplets were out, but Parker's team still had to answer this correctly to officially win. Ms. Garcia barely had a chance to read the question again to her team before Parker blurted out, "Three percent is freshwater!"

Cassie jumped up and hugged her. Even Theo smiled a little bit.

The first event of the Science Triathlon was theirs! It was one small step to becoming a world-famous scientist. And it hadn't been easy.

Parker had known that some of the other teams would be just as prepared as hers. The Dempsey Triplets had taken her completely by surprise, though.

Aidan and Braidan and Jaidan made fart noises

all the time. They also planned a lot of pranks that didn't work.

Just a couple of weeks ago, Braidan and Jaidan had tried to hold their breath under water by putting their noses into their thermoses. They hadn't believed Aidan when he told them that even if their noses were under water, they could still breathe through their mouths.

Now that Parker thought about it, it made sense that Aidan had slayed the Science Bee without any help from his brothers.

All this time Parker had been worried that Theo was going to be her biggest problem in the Science Triathlon. Now she knew the truth.

Her team had some fierce scientific competition.

Chapter 5

The Friendship Experiment

While there was no big announcement in science the next day, there were still some surprises.

To start, Ms. Garcia asked all the Science Triathlon teams to come in from recess a few minutes early for a quick meeting. When Parker came back in, there was a box of drinking straws sitting on her desk. But that wasn't all. Someone had thought it was a good idea to give the Dempsey Triplets duct tape.

Parker figured Ms. Garcia must have left it out by accident. No teacher would make the mistake of giving these boys duct tape.

They were already ripping off strips of the stuff and taping their mouths shut.

It was going to be a *lo-o-o-ong* meeting after all.

It turned out that Ms. Garcia hadn't left the duct

tape out by accident. She'd done it completely on purpose. She even passed out more rolls to the other teams.

No one else taped their teammates' mouths shut.

"The next event in the Science Triathlon is the Egg Drop!" Ms. Garcia said as she pulled tape off Braidan's mouth. "Each team will get a box of straws and some heavy-duty tape." *Ri-i-i-i-i-ip.* The tape came off Jaidan, too. "And from just those two things, you'll have to create a case that will protect your egg when I drop it off the school's roof." Ms. Garcia zipped the tape off Aidan's mouth. All three Dempsey Triplets had red rectangles on the skin around their mouths where the duct tape had been.

Parker looked away from them when Jaidan crossed his eyes and stuck his tongue out at her.

The Dempsey Triplets never seemed to be interested in school. And yet they somehow had come in second place in the Science Bee.

From a scientific point of view, Parker wanted to know how that had happened. When had Aidan found enough time to study for the Science Bee with all the goofing off he did? And how had he done so well in the Science Bee while his brothers had sat around and made fart noises?

Parker focused as Ms. Garcia explained what they had to achieve in the Egg Drop.

"Whenever there's a force acting on an object, there's acceleration," Ms. Garcia said. "And in this case, the force is gravity pulling your egg down to the ground."

That all made sense to Parker. The egg would move faster as it fell.

"But it's not the acceleration of gravity that will break your egg," Ms. Garcia continued. "It's the negative acceleration when the egg stops very quickly and hits the ground."

"SPLAT!" called out Braidan. Jaidan pretended to be an egg exploding. Parker shook her head at them.

"So what each team needs to do is figure out how to slow down the velocity of your egg as it drops from the roof so that the splat doesn't happen when the egg lands," Ms. Garcia said.

As she explained that they were not allowed to use any other materials for this project, Parker was thinking hard. Even though her team had won the Science Bee, there was still a lot of work to do on the next two Triathlon events. Clearly it wasn't going to be easy to prove they were the best scientists. The Dempseys were a bigger threat than they had let on. And they weren't the only other strong team in the competition.

Walking in the footsteps of Jane and Mae was harder than Parker had thought it would be.

She and Cassie and Theo had to keep working.

Thankfully, Parker was very good at making gadgets and gizmos. So the Egg Drop would be easy-peasy. All she had to do was organize her team and get to work in her Mad Science Lab, and she knew they would be able to come up with a fierce Egg Drop contender.

o   o   o

It turned out that organizing her team was going to be harder than Parker had thought.

Cassie had two soccer games that week because last week's had been rained out. She also really wanted to go to Mara's gymnastics competition, which was this week too.

Trying to plan was getting frustrating.

"Well, what days are you around to work on the Egg Drop, Theo?" Parker asked, with a little bit of that frustration in her voice.

Theo shrugged.

"Not Wednesday, right?" Cassie said. "We have Coders' Club after school."

Parker did not like being reminded that Cassie and Theo were in a club together. Or that Parker didn't have any club to go to, with her best friend or otherwise.

Besides, they had bigger problems right now.

They couldn't even find a day to get together after school to prepare for the next event in the Triathlon.

By the time Parker got home and plunked down at a table in her dad's bakery, she was tired. She was feeling a little left out. She was *exasperated.*

Then she looked up and saw something that made her feel not only exasperated but just plain shocked.

Theo was standing at the counter *talking to her dad!*

Parker watched him. His mouth opened and closed. Words came out. Theo wasn't turning red or whispering. Something he said even made her dad laugh.

Which meant that Theo could talk to a cat, her dad, and even a teeny bit to Cassie. For some reason, though, he wouldn't talk to Parker. Something had to be done about this.

With five quick steps, Parker was at the counter.

She got there just in time to hear Theo talking about the price of eggs.

Eggs? Why on earth would he be talking to her dad about eggs? Or how much they cost?

Theo turned around and saw Parker staring at him. His mouth stopped opening and closing. No more words about eggs or anything else came out. Instead, his face turned as red as Parker had ever seen it.

"Hi," Parker said, trying to break the ice.

"Hi," Theo said back in the quietest possible voice.

"Theo, are you ready?" a man called from the bakery door.

Her Triathlon teammate gave a nod but didn't say anything. He did wave goodbye, though, as they left the bakery.

She turned to her dad. "I can't believe you got him to talk," she said.

Her dad smiled. "We chat whenever he and his dad come in."

"Then why won't he talk to me?" she asked. Parker was starting to feel more than exasperated. Now her feelings were hurt. Theo might want to be friends with Cassie, but he clearly didn't want to be friends with Parker.

Her dad scrunched up his eyebrows as he thought it over. "Maybe he's just shy," he said at last. "Maybe he's like Ultra-Megabot in Morph-Bots. He's powerful but quiet."

Parker stopped to consider that. Ultra-Megabot was the strongest of all the Morph-Bots robots. He could morph into ten different kinds of robot depending on what kind of situations the characters got themselves into. One of the forms he took was the giant robotic eagle that was on Parker's backpack.

"But all the other robots know Ultra-Megabot is the best," Parker said. "And he's not really *that* quiet. He gave a huge speech before the Battle of Morph Mountain."

"True," her dad said. "But in the beginning, he

didn't give speeches and no one could see that he'd be able to take on the Terrorbots."

"So you're saying that Theo is going to defeat a swarm of evil robots?"

Her dad laughed as he handed her one of his famous chocolate chip cookies. "I'm saying you should give him a chance."

Parker went back to her table and munched on her cookie. Maybe her dad was right. Maybe Theo was a Ultra-Megabot in hiding. Or Peter Parker before he turned into Spider-Man.

She had lots of proof that Theo Zachary could actually talk, after all. She'd seen it with her own eyes. She had even heard a little bit of it with her own ears.

But one question still bothered her: If Theo could talk, why wouldn't he talk to her?

An idea started brewing in her brain. She could use a scientific method of inquiry to figure out how to get Theo to talk to her. Since Theo talked only to

Cassie, maybe he was trying to steal her BFF! The thought hadn't occurred to Parker until now, but it made sense. This was getting serious.

Parker whipped out her notebook and started to write.

INITIAL QUESTION: Why does Theo Zachary talk to Cassie, Cleopatra, and even Dad, but not me? And why does he especially talk to Cassie?

BRAINSTORM SOLUTIONS: Cassie is nice to Theo, so he wants to talk to her.

GATHER DATA: Cassie did not freak out when Theo sat in our seat on the bus. Or every time he keeps sitting in it. She also asked him to be on our Science Triathlon team (without even asking me!). Then they designed a game together.

USE DATA TO MAKE A PREDICTION: If I try to be super friendly to him, he will like me more and will talk to me. Then Cassie will remain my BFF and Theo can be a secondary kind of friend.

Parker would have to see how her predictions

panned out before she could communicate her results, of course. But she had a bad feeling that by the end of her experiment she'd end up with proof that Theo didn't want to be her friend no matter how nice she was to him.

Chapter 6

Flying the Coop

Parker Bell sometimes had a hard time believing that she and her mom were related. It wasn't just that her mom always wore sweatpants. Or that she was more interested in basketball than science. It wasn't even that she and her mom didn't look anything alike. It was that her mom didn't understand that she sometimes got Parker into tricky situations.

"That sounds great," her mom said into the phone. "I can drop Parker off tomorrow at two o'clock."

"Drop me off where?" Parker whispered, but her mom waved her off.

"Is there anything she can bring?" Parker's mom said. After a long pause, Parker saw her mom smile. "Perfect. She'll see you then."

"Who will see me then?" Parker asked. "Where

am I supposed to be going in the middle of a perfectly good Saturday afternoon?"

"To Theo's house to work on your Egg Drop project," her mom told her. "Cassie's going too. Theo's dad said you didn't need to bring anything, but I think they'd like some of Dad's lemon drop cookies, don't you?"

Parker dropped down onto a kitchen chair in a huff. "Why did you say yes?" she asked.

Her mom sat across from her. "Because you need to get ready for the Egg Drop," she replied. "I thought you'd be happy there's finally time for you three to work together."

"No, I am, but . . ."

"But what, honey?"

"I wanted to work here in my Mad Science Lab," Parker said. "What if there's no room there to create anything? Or if Theo's parents try to make the Egg Drop case for us? Some parents are like that, you know." Parker clunked her forehead down onto the table. "What happens when Cassie has to use the bathroom and Theo just sits there not talking to me?"

"Is that what you're worried about?" her mom asked. "Theo not talking to you?"

Parker took a deep breath and sat up again. She decided to tell her mom about what had been going on. "I don't think Theo wants to be friends with me," Parker blurted out. "And I'm not sure *I* want to be friends with him. I just want to work with Cassie in my lab!"

Her mom took her hand. "It's good to have more than one friend," her mom said. "It's like the robot thingies. You can never have too many."

Parker knew her mom was trying, but calling the Morph-Bots "robot thingies"? Besides, her mom had two sisters, a million friends at the high school where she worked, *and* Parker's dad. She didn't understand what it was like to have just one super-important friend.

"Why don't you go to Theo's and see how it goes?" her mom suggested.

"Okay," Parker said. She knew what this meant: she was being forced to start testing her theory about Theo on his own turf. Or, as her PE teacher mom would have put it, Parker had lost the home court advantage. And she didn't like it one bit.

o   o   o

"It's not going to be that bad," Cassie whispered to her in the back of Parker's mom's car the next day. "You should see him at Coders' Club. He's really smart. You should give him a chance."

Parker was ready to give Theo a chance. Even if she didn't really want to be friends with him, she had to get to the bottom of why *he* didn't want to be friends with *her.* If nothing else, she was doing it for the sake of scientific inquiry. Well, and also to make sure he wasn't going to steal her BFF.

Parker had her prediction. Now she had to see if it would yield any results.

By the time they got to Theo's house, she was in full-on science mode. She rang the doorbell ready for anything.

A tall, skinny man with big ears just like Theo's greeted them with a smile. Theo looked up and whispered something to his dad.

"You must be Parker and Cassie!" he said. "I'm Theo's dad, Tim. I'm so glad his new science buddies could come over today."

Now Parker was confused. Sure, this man looked like Theo. And Parker had read a lot about how genes work, so she knew that he and Theo had to have some of the same ones. But Theo's dad talked a lot. He had a good, loud voice, too.

It was the weirdest thing ever.

"Come on inside and have a snack before you start working," Theo's dad said, taking the bakery box from Parker. "I have a feeling these are going to inspire you guys to eggy greatness!"

Suddenly, Parker knew what was going on here.

Theo and his dad were like her and her mom. They were genetically related, but they weren't a whole lot alike.

The discovery that she and Theo might actually have something in common made her feel a little less nervous about being at his house. It also inspired her to eat three cookies, two more than she'd be allowed to have at home. She needed fuel to keep her brain going, after all.

When they got to Theo's room, Parker stopped short. Theo might not necessarily *be* like Ultra-Megabot, but he had posters of him all around his bedroom. One was the same picture of Ultra-Megabot as a giant eagle-bot that Parker had on her backpack.

It was time to begin her experiment by being extra-super friendly to Theo. "You like Morph-Bots too?" she asked him. She remembered Cassie had told her this, but she hadn't realized how much he liked them.

He nodded really fast. "Love them," he said. He said something! Scientific inquiry rocked!

Parker looked at Cassie, but Cassie was wearing her very best *I told you so* look on her face. She was also wearing her very best Terrorbots T-shirt under a purple plaid shirt. Parker never could understand why Cassie liked the bad guys so much, but she did like Cassie's personal style.

She also liked Theo's huge shelf of Morph-Bots action figures. He had tons of Megabots and even a few Terrorbots. They were set up as if they were about to battle it out. The Terrorbots looked like they were going to lose. Badly.

"Wow, you have so many!" Parker said. "I only have three and they're all different forms of Ultra-Megabot."

"My mom works for Morph-Bots," Theo said. They were the most words she'd ever heard him say at once, and he'd said them to her.

"Oh. My. Morph-Bots." Parker couldn't believe

her ears. Her experiment was yielding the best results ever! "Will she come home while we're here? I have so many questions to ask her!"

With that, Theo turned red and lost all his words again. Parker wasn't sure what she had done wrong. Or maybe it was her scientific testing that wasn't going right? Maybe being friendly wasn't the key to getting Theo to talk after all? She was kerflummoxed.

Cassie gasped out loud, and Parker immediately turned to make sure she was okay. Her BFF actually looked thrilled. Something had caught her eye outside.

"You have chickens!" Cassie exclaimed. "Can we go meet them?"

"Sure," Theo said. He didn't even whisper or mumble.

"Okay, let's do it!" Cassie sounded really excited. Theo looked really excited.

Parker Bell was not excited. She was trying so hard to be extra-super friendly to Theo to prove her prediction about him talking as part of her experiment, but this was going too far.

"I hate chickens," she whispered to Cassie as they walked outside.

"Theo was really good with Cleopatra," Cassie told her. "Maybe he's really good with other animals, too. Maybe his chickens are amazing."

Theo's chickens were not amazing. As he led Parker and Cassie into the chicken enclosure and shut the gate behind them, Parker made some scientific observations. The chickens smelled like puke. They made weird noises. And they had those bony, yucky feet that all chickens have.

Parker still really hated chickens.

Theo, on the other hand, clearly loved them.

"Come here, girls," he called to them. The chickens all came running.

"Here, you can feed them," he said to Cassie in a quiet voice. Theo put some chicken feed into Cassie's hand, and the chickens ate right from her palm.

He gave some to Parker, too, but he didn't say a

word. He didn't even look at her. Parker took the feed and crouched down by the chickens.

That was a big mistake.

The chickens surrounded her, trying to peck at her hand to get the food. She panicked and dumped it all, but some of it fell onto her foot.

The chickens were closing in on her. They all began pecking at her feet. She couldn't swat them away.

"ARGH!" Parker fell backward onto her behind as a chicken pooped on her favorite gold shoes.

Just as she seemed lost in a sea of crazed hens, Theo stepped in front of her and put his hand out. She took it and he pulled her up.

Theo had saved her from the evil chickens. For once, Parker was the one who didn't know what to say.

"Um . . . th-thanks," Parker sputtered out.

He glanced at her and even sort of smiled. "No problem," he said.

Sure, she was covered in chicken crud. And she'd

have to take a bath to end all baths that night. But Theo had just willingly talked to her.

Maybe her friendship experiment would work after all. Maybe he would start talking to her all the time now.

Which was good. Because they still had to face the Egg Drop, and they were going to have to work together to have a real chance at winning.

Chapter 7

Eureka!

Even though Parker slayed at building contraptions and gadgets, her teammates wouldn't let her design the Egg Drop case on her own.

"We're a team, so we have to come up with the idea together," Cassie said. "Something fun and cool to look at. Like a really well-made video game."

"We also have to make sure it's safe," Theo said.

"Safe?" Cassie asked.

Even though Theo turned a little red, he still answered. "Eggs are important," he said. "We can't let ours break."

This was going nowhere fast. Cassie wanted a cool design. Theo had a thing about chickens. And now that Parker was being extra-super nice to him, he was even talking about his thing for chickens. She had to find a way to get the team to start working.

"Maybe designing something to keep the egg safe is kind of like designing online games," Parker said. "Where do you start with making a game, Theo?"

"First you have to figure out what kind of game you want to make," Theo replied. "Then you have to decide what the rules of the game are."

"You also have to brainstorm how to find the best way to make the rules work," Cassie added.

"Then you can start thinking about how to code it so that it all comes together," Theo said. He was really talking now!

"So, in the trivia game, you had to figure out how to ask the questions and give out the prizes to build up Ultra-Megabot, right?"

Cassie's eyes lighted up at the mention of her trivia game. "Right!" Cassie said. "But I had to try it lots of different ways before I got it to work."

"We have to do the same thing here. That's how science works too!" Parker said. "The Egg Drop is about velocity. The egg'll fall off the school building *fast* because gravity pulls at it. So, to keep the egg safe" — she turned to Theo — "we have to slow it down as it drops off the school roof. And then make sure it lands as gently as possible."

"Let's come up with a list of possible ideas on how the tape and straws can slow the egg down," Cassie said. "Then we can vote on which one to try."

They looked at one of Theo's chickens' eggs to get ideas. They talked and made lists of how the materials they had to work with might slow down the egg's velocity. They played around with the straws and duct tape to explore their properties.

What they didn't do was come up with a single plan.

The doorbell rang, and Parker knew it was her mom here to pick up her and Cassie. Sure, Parker had thought they were doomed once or twice before. Now they really were. A whole afternoon was gone and they still didn't even have any plan for their case.

Parker was starting to lose her cool. She took a

deep breath. Sometimes the best scientific ideas came from the simplest of places. Like Alexander Fleming accidentally finding a mold that turned out to be penicillin. Or Archimedes stepping into his bathtub, watching the water rise, and yelling, "Eureka!" as he made a sudden discovery about water density.

Parker needed a eureka moment. She needed some inspiration!

What can slow down as it travels through the air? First she thought of an airplane, but that slowed down because of the engines and the wings.

The wings!

Looking up, she saw her backpack out of the corner of her eye. The same picture was on Theo's wall, too: Ultra-Megabot soaring through the sky like an eagle.

"That's it!" Parker said.

"What's it?" Cassie asked.

Parker pointed to the poster on Theo's wall. "Ultra-Megabot," she said. "We should make an egg case that soars like an eagle!"

Cassie's eyes widened. Theo smiled the biggest smile Parker had ever seen on his face.

"With wings?" he asked.

"Of course," Parker said. "Duct tape–covered straw wings. The wings will slow down the velocity of the egg as it drops."

"And we'll need a box like an eagle's body to keep the egg safe," Cassie said, looking at Theo.

"That egg is never even going to come close to crashing on the ground," Parker told him. She was being friendly, getting him to talk, *and* coming up with amazing scientific ideas. They were totally going to win the gold medal. She was going to be just like Jane and Mae!

Cassie called her dad to ask if she could stay longer, and Parker's mom agreed to come back for the two girls later. The three teammates dug back in. There were straws everywhere. Duct tape stuck to every surface in Theo's room. Like Cassie's online trivia game, they had to think about what they wanted and how best to make it. Should the body of their eagle be round? Oval? Square? What shape should the wings be? Did the whole thing need a tail of straws like a real bird had a tail of feathers? Little by little, they had their case.

It was a tiny box made of straws cut in half, held together at the seams with duct tape so the case wasn't too rigid and would keep the egg safe and sound. Attached were two wings made of full-length straws completely covered in duct tape.

The teammates even made a tiny eagle head and colored it in Ultra-Megabot's red, purple, and blue.

"Fierce," Parker and Cassie said at the same time.

Theo smiled. "Definitely." He seemed happy and was talking so much more than Parker had ever expected when she'd begun her Theo experiment.

One question still nagged at Parker, though. Would Theo keep on talking if her idea for the egg case didn't protect the very important egg inside? Or would their little scrap of a friendship crash-land along with the yolk? Since Theo's dad wouldn't let them climb up to the roof of the house to drop their creation as a trial run, Parker was going to have to wait until Egg Drop day to find out.

o   o   o

Egg Drop day was there before they knew it. Ms. Garcia was on the roof of Eleanor Roosevelt Elementary School, while Principal Warren hung out with the Science Triathlon teams on the ground.

Parker held her breath when Ms. Garcia held the first case over the edge of the roof and let go. The container looked like it had a duct tape parachute attached. At first, the taped-up chute even acted like a real one, slowing down the egg.

Then, disaster struck. One of the straps of the parachute broke and the whole contraption crashed to the ground. Egg guts oozed out onto the sidewalk.

"What do you call an egg that breaks its parachute?" Aidan asked. No one answered.

"Scrambled!" he said.

Jaidan and Braidan laughed as if it was the

funniest thing they'd ever heard. Even Parker had to admit it was a pretty good joke. But it would have been much better if it wasn't about someone's scientific and design work.

Theo frowned and looked away from the smashed egg. He clearly didn't enjoy egg jokes at all, even if they weren't about his egg.

"Just ignore them," Parker whispered to him.

The next egg case came flying down from the roof. It looked like there was almost no duct tape holding the little box of straws together. The whole thing hit the ground with a splat.

"What happened when the egg case hit the ground?" Aidan asked.

Cassie sighed. Parker shot him a nasty look. Aidan didn't seem to notice.

"It egg-sploded!" he said. "Get it, Parker? Egg-sploded?"

"That's just rude," Parker said to him. "Don't make fun of people's egg cases." Even if some of her fellow students clearly didn't understand what it meant to slow down the egg's velocity, no one deserved to get teased about it.

Aidan grinned at her. "You sound like you're getting eggs-asperated with me, Parker," he said.

Parker couldn't argue with him there. She *was* getting exasperated. And she wasn't even in the classroom, where she could calm herself down by watching Snodgrass devour crickets.

Instead, she focused on Ms. Garcia holding another egg case over the edge of the roof. The third-place Science Bee girls from Mr. Tanner's class held on to one another's arms as they watched their case fall.

This one seemed like a huge cube made out of lots of straws and duct tape. It looked *strong*.

It came down fast and hit the ground with a thud, but there was no egg ooze that Parker could see. The girls picked up their cube. The egg inside had a very small dent on its shell, but otherwise it had stayed together.

Parker was happy for them, of course. She was

also worried about her team's Egg Drop case. What if they smashed up Theo's precious egg and then the Dempseys somehow were the ones to clinch the gold medal? What if losing the Triathlon made Theo stop talking to her again? And what would it say about her as a scientist if the Dempseys had made a better contraption than her own team had? Nothing good, she was afraid.

"That was almost an egg-cellent drop!" Aidan Dempsey called to the girls from Mr. Tanner's class.

At least he was being nicer this time. It was more than could be said for his fellow triplets, who were making crunching, cracking noises. And the

egg hadn't even made a noise when its shell had dented.

Another disaster followed. "If we keep breaking eggs like this, they might go egg-stinct!" Aidan said with a guffaw. Jaidan and Braidan laughed so hard that they fell onto the ground.

Principal Warren asked them to behave, and about time!

They kept snickering to themselves, though. That is, until Ms. Garcia held up their egg case. It looked like a drinking straw porcupine. Hoards of straws came out like spines from a little straw box in the middle. It was a fierce design. This was too bad, as Parker had fully planned to lay an egg joke on the triplets when their case crashed on the ground.

When it dropped, the case worked perfectly. It slowed down the velocity of the egg and gave it a great cushion when the container hit the ground with all of its negative acceleration glory. Aidan rushed over to pick up the porcupine and held it gently in his hands.

Parker watched him as he took the egg out of its case. There wasn't even a tiny crack on it. Aidan was clearly a secret science genius hiding under rude egg jokes and hand farts.

Then Ms. Garcia held Parker, Cassie, and Theo's case over the edge of the roof and let go. It kicked right into gear, but not in the way Parker's team had expected. Instead of soaring like Ultra-Megabot and slowly decelerating until the egg descended to the ground like an airplane, the wings made the whole contraption spin like a helicopter's propeller. Sure, this slowed down the egg case's fall. But it also made the container catch the wind and travel out of the schoolyard and into the hedges.

Were the wings the wrong length? This was what came of not testing their design ahead of time and being able to make tweaks to it, Parker realized.

"That was eggs-barrassing!" joked Jaidan.

Parker was not amused.

Just as she was about to tell him so, Aidan of all people beat her to it. "That doesn't even make sense, Jaidan," he told him.

Parker was so shocked, she didn't know what to say.

"Your egg case was good," he said to her. "But maybe it needed to be wider in the wingspan?" Parker couldn't believe that he also thought it was a problem with the length of the wings.

"Um, yours was good too," Parker replied. Better than her team's case, even. She'd have to think more about the wingspan thing.

But first, Cassie was pulling her and Theo away to get their egg container.

While they were gone, the Dempsey Triplets were declared the winner of the Egg Drop. Parker, Cassie, and Theo didn't even come in second.

"Technically, your contraption didn't hit the ground," Ms. Garcia told Parker. "So there was no way to prove that it would have offset the negative acceleration."

Despite all their hard work, their case hadn't worked properly. Sure, their egg was still in one piece, so at least Theo wouldn't be mad about it breaking. But since the container never touched the ground, they'd never know if it really would have protected the egg or not. How was Parker ever going to be like Jane and Mae if she couldn't even win an Egg Drop?

Chapter 8

Not Enough Data

They were down to the wire. Almost at the finish line. The Animal Adaptation Presentations were near.

Parker had one last chance to become an award-winning scientist like Jane and Mae. And she was also running out of time to test her predictions about Theo. There was surprisingly a lot on the line for the last Science Triathlon event.

Cassie and even Theo seemed to feel the same way. The whole team wanted to do their best science. First, they had to figure out a topic for their presentation. As they sat on the bus together, they talked it through.

Theo was still sitting in the sixth row on the left, in Parker and Cassie's seat. Parker minded this a little bit less as the Science Triathlon went on. She and Cassie sat in front of him now. The fifth row wasn't as bad as Parker had thought it would be, really. It was practically like sitting in the sixth.

Cassie had her notebook out to capture all of their good ideas.

"What about snakes?" Cassie said. "The ones that live in the desert don't have to drink a lot of water to survive. I have a whole book about it."

"But how could we do any science about desert snakes?" Parker asked. "We can't get a desert snake to study on such short notice."

"We could make a tri-fold poster," Cassie said. "With pictures."

"We could," Parker replied. "But making a poster wouldn't be real science. We lost the Egg Drop, so we have to step it up with our presentation. It can't just be *about* science. It has to show our mad science *skills.*"

Theo opened his mouth but no words came out.

"What is it?" Parker asked him. She thought she

was being friendly and involving him, but he winced when she asked.

He shook his head. The girls went back to brainstorming.

"I mean, we could do monarch butterflies," Cassie said.

"I bet other teams will do monarchs," Parker replied. "We need something different."

"Unique!" Cassie added.

"Extraordinary!" Parker said with a smile.

Theo seemed like he wanted to say something again, but instead he looked out the window. Parker had thought he was warming up to her. She had even begun to think that together they might be like the three angles of a triangle, always adding up to a perfect 180 degrees. But when it came to their Animal Adaptation Presentation, Theo's talking had come to a dead stop.

"What about emperor penguins living in Antarctica?" Cassie suggested. "And how they learned to huddle together to stay warm?"

Cassie loved penguins, so Parker had to think this one through. How could they make a penguin presentation amazing and oozing with science?

She couldn't come up with a single way.

"We'd still only have a tri-fold, though," she told her BFF. "We need a topic that we can do real science with. Or even some engineering!" Engineering was what her dad called her robotic guinea pig feeder. And the book holder she'd built for her mom, to apologize for taking apart the toaster (and that she had made with the leftover toaster parts that she hadn't used for her guinea pig feeder). Engineering probably also applied to the arm she'd made in her Mad Science Lab to swab gross things onto petri dishes.

Turned out that Parker had loved engineering for ages without even knowing it had a name.

But that still didn't help her come up with a good idea for their presentation.

"You guys can't even come up with a project, can you?" called Braidan from the back of the bus. "Too bad!"

"So sad!" Jaidan called.

"'Cause we're going to win!" Braidan said. He and Jaidan burst out laughing. They weren't laughing with Parker and her friends, though. They were laughing at them.

One of the many things that got Parker peeved was being laughed at. Especially when she was being laughed at by the two nonscientific Dempsey Triplets.

As Braidan and Jaidan went back to trying to make convincing pig noises, Parker tried to think. It was time to rally her team. They were smart. They were creative. They were maybe-kind-of-sort-of a perfect triangle.

They could do this.

"You guys, ignore them," Parker told her friends. "They wouldn't know a good animal adaptation if it hit them on the head."

"All they think about is farts," Cassie agreed.

"And they tell terrible jokes," Theo said in a quiet

voice. The jokes from Egg Drop day had clearly stayed with him. Theo did love eggs and chickens.

"So all we need to do is pick an animal and figure out how to wow Principal Warren with our science when she judges the presentations."

Theo cleared his throat and turned bright red.

"Um, we could do chickens," he said.

Parker's eyebrows went high up on her forehead. Her eyes bugged out. If Grandma Bell were here, she definitely would warn Parker about having her face stick that way. (Even though Parker really had told her over and over that scientifically it couldn't happen.)

"That's a great idea!" Cassie said as she wrote in her notebook.

Not only was Theo bringing his dreaded chickens into the picture, but Parker's own BFF thought it was a good idea.

"But I hate chickens!" Parker protested. "You know I do."

Cassie didn't look up from her writing. "I know,

but sometimes you have to sacrifice for science," she told Parker. "And we need to pick an animal for our presentation!"

"We could bring in one of my chickens," Theo said. "And even a chick if one hatches in time, so we can talk about the down and how it keeps the chicks warm."

Now that Theo had started talking about chickens, there was no stopping him. Parker wasn't sure if that proved or disproved her prediction about being kind to get him to talk. There was a strong possibility her prediction was wrong. Parker hadn't considered that Theo might talk only when he was excited about something, like coding or chickens. Maybe he talked to Cassie because they shared lots of interests. All he and Parker had in common was their love of Morph-Bots. She needed to reassess her predictions.

She also needed to get this situation under control.

"I'm sure we can't bring live animals to school," said Parker.

"But there already is a live animal in our classroom," Cassie said.

"And all the crickets that Snodgrass eats are alive too," Theo added.

Parker had to think, and she had to think fast. They just couldn't do chickens for the Animal Adaptation Presentation! They couldn't do chickens at all! Chickens were one of the top ten things that got Parker peeved. And by "peeved," Parker really meant *scared her like crazy.*

Besides, if they did chickens, how would Parker ever know if Theo was talking more because he loved the animals or because she was being nice to him? There were now too many variables to know if her experiment proved anything or not.

"Snodgrass is in a tank," she told them, thinking fast. "The chicken won't be. It will just poop all over school, and we'll end up in trouble."

Finally, Cassie looked up from her notebook. "Parker, you've said no to every idea that we've come up with." Cassie did not sound pleased. "And you haven't come up with any ideas of your own."

"So maybe we can do chickens?" Theo said.

"We're not doing chickens!" Parker exclaimed. "We can't just bring in an animal. We need to do real science if we're going to win!" She had this one chance to prove to the world she was a real scientist, like Jane and Mae. She wasn't going to blow it now.

"Then what are we going to do?" Theo asked.

It was a good question. Just not one that Parker had the data to answer.

Chapter 9

Some Guinea Pig

Parker went home feeling discouraged. Her mom had a headache from dodge ball day in her PE classes. Her dad was super busy in the bakery. So Parker went to the one living creature in the house she knew was always there for her and always understood exactly how she was feeling: Algebra.

Her guinea pig hopped out of his cage and walked around for a bit, stretching out his itty-bitty legs. Then he climbed into Parker's lap.

"You're some guinea pig, you know that, Algebra?" Parker said. "Much better than chickens."

The furry little guy climbed up to Parker's shoulder and nestled there, as if he really understood how much Parker needed him right then.

Parker scratched behind his ears, and Algebra purred like a little engine.

"Like a little engine!" Parker said under her breath. She reached up and took the piggy off her shoulder.

Suddenly, Parker was having a eureka moment all over again.

Parker looked at Algebra very carefully. Itty-bitty legs. Beady eyes. Compact size. He could run fast to escape predators, even though there weren't any in Parker's bedroom. He could squeak, really loudly sometimes, as if he was trying to communicate with her. The wild cousins of guinea pigs weren't exactly just like her domestic little guy, but they did the same thing to talk to one another. And if he were female, he could have a zillion babies to make sure that guinea pigs reigned supreme forever.

He was one amazing bundle of animal adaptations.

The guinea pig kept purring and Parker felt so happy that she could purr herself.

She finally had the perfect solution to the chicken problem. But just bringing Algebra into class wasn't going to win her team a gold medal. They had to go above and beyond and really prove themselves as scientists to win the Triathlon. Besides, she really didn't think Ms. Garcia would like it if they brought a live animal to school, especially for an all-school assembly. What Parker had to do was figure out how to make one guinea pig into an amazing and really scientific presentation.

But no brilliant ideas were popping into her head. She collapsed onto her bed, holding Algebra in her arms.

Parker looked up at Jane and Mae.

"You two would know how to make this happen," she said glumly. "But I can't figure it out at all."

Jane looked like she completely understood. Mae smiled as if she fully believed Parker could do this. She hoped Mae was right.

o   o   o

The best idea ever came to Parker when she least expected it: over the macaroni and cheese her dad had made for dinner. Oh, it wasn't the mac and cheese that made the long-lasting LED light bulb go off inside her head. It was the double-armed robot in the middle of the kitchen table that she'd built last year. One arm held the saltshaker, the other the pepper. All you had to do was press a button in front of your plate and the robot would swivel around and bring you whichever shaker you wanted. Even her mom had been impressed with this gadget (probably because Parker hadn't taken apart anything in the kitchen to make it).

Parker loved robots. She had heaps and hoards of robotic parts and engines and kits in her Mad Science Lab. Enough to do something really brilliant for the Animal Adaptation Presentation. Something brilliant like building a guinea pig robot!

But Parker wouldn't be able to show off all of Algebra's many animal adaptations with a single robot. She needed to think bigger than that. She needed to *build* bigger than that. Her team wasn't going to make just one robot.

"We're going to make a whole robot army!" she announced during dinner.

Her mom and dad looked over at her. "You're going to make a what?" her mom asked.

"A robot army," Parker replied. "Of guinea pigs. For the Animal Adaptation Presentation. That way, even if we don't win, we can still chase off the Dempsey Triplets with our robotic minions!" This idea was getting better by the minute!

Her mom and dad stopped eating. They looked at each other. Then they looked back at Parker.

"No," her dad said. "No way."

"Why?" Parker cried. "You don't think I'd be able to do it?"

"No, honey, we think you *would* be able to do it," her mom said. "That's the problem."

"Robotic minions are never a good idea," said

her dad. "They always lead to trouble in the movies. Don't you remember what happened in *Robot Alive*?"

"The minions ate all the people," her mom offered. "I didn't even know robots could eat people."

"I guess some can," her dad replied.

"But that was just a movie," Parker reminded them. "This is real life. Real robots don't eat people. They don't eat anything. They just use power."

"Power they get from eating people," her dad said.

Parker couldn't tell if they were joking or if that movie had had a stronger impact on her parents than she'd thought. Personally, she had found it unrealistic.

"Well, our robot army won't eat people," Parker declared.

"They'll just chase off the Dempsey Triplets?" her mom said.

"Only if Aidan and Braidan and Jaidan don't take the last part of the Science Triathlon seriously enough," Parker replied.

Her parents looked at each other again. "No way," they said at the same time.

Parker sighed. "What if I promised that we wouldn't go after the Dempsey Triplets with our guinea pigs?"

Her dad twisted his mouth into his thinking expression. "And the robots wouldn't eat anyone?"

"The only thing they'd do is show off guinea pig adaptations," Parker promised. "No eating anyone or chasing anyone."

Her dad looked at her mom and her mom looked at her dad. "Sounds like some gold medal science to me," her mom said.

"Especially with Cassie and Theo to help you," her dad added.

Parker's face clouded over.

"What's wrong?" her dad asked. "You're still working with Cassie and Theo, right?"

"I only just thought of the idea," Parker told him. "All I have to do is let them know and we can start building."

But a tiny bit of worry poked at her the way Jaidan's finger had all last year in art. What if Cassie and Theo didn't agree to her brilliant idea? What if they ended up doing chickens?

What if Parker never got a chance to prove what a good scientist she was by winning the gold medal?

Chapter 10

Mad Scientists at Work

Parker always did her best scientific work in her lab. She'd built a two-foot-tall Ultra-Megabot in there. She regularly examined things like her own hair and guinea pig poop with her microscope. She constructed contraptions using the bins of tools and petri dishes and spare parts that lined the lab. She never threw anything away, as who knew when she'd need leftover robotic spider legs or a mini solar panel or even old wires to connect the things she built to their power sources.

Her Mad Science Lab was the best room in the whole house. And it was all hers!

For the next few afternoons, though, it would be Cassie's and Theo's, too. Cassie didn't love the Mad Science Lab the way Parker did, because Cassie was more into computers and facts than working out experiments and building. None of that mattered now, though. Parker had everything they needed all in this one room to make the very best, most scientific Animal Adaptation Presentation ever.

All she had to do was convince Cassie and Theo to build the army of guinea pig bots.

"So here's what I've been thinking . . ." Parker began. That was as far as she got, though. Because Theo had something to say.

"Wow!" For once, Theo wasn't looking at his shoes. He walked around Parker's lab, looking at everything. "This is the best room ever."

"Thanks!" Parker said. "It's my favorite too."

"Are these all robot parts?" Theo asked, peeking into a bin.

"Yep," Parker said. "And did you see the Ultra-Megabot I made? It can talk in his voice, or you can record your own so he sounds like you."

Theo picked up the robot and admired it. "This is amazing."

It turned out that the Mad Science Lab brought out the new talking Theo. And it turned out that Parker and Theo had more in common than she'd thought. Just as Parker opened her mouth to say more friendly things (what better place to keep testing out her theory about Theo than in an actual lab?), Cassie reminded them why they were there.

"Should we brainstorm presentation ideas?" Cassie said. "The sooner we get started, the better!"

"Yes!" Parker replied, getting back on topic. "Let's do this."

Cassie tossed her long braid over her shoulder and got out her notebook so she could write everything down. "Who's got an idea of what we should do?" she asked.

At the very same moment, Parker, Cassie, and the new talking Theo all blurted out answers.

"Guinea pigs!" Parker said.

"Cats!" Cassie said.

"Chickens!" Theo said.

They all looked at one another for a second.

"Okay, that's a lot of ideas," said Cassie. "So which do we do?"

That turned out to be a tricky question.

"What could our project be if we did cats?" Parker asked Cassie. Parker wanted to do guinea pigs, of course. But Cassie was her BFF, so Parker needed to take her ideas seriously.

Cassie bit her lip as she thought about it. "Well, we couldn't bring Cleopatra, even if there wasn't a live animal issue," she replied. "Cleo would *freak out* around so many people."

"I guess we could make a cat poster," Theo ventured.

Parker wanted to remind him that a poster was a boring idea, but then she had to remind herself that she was being extra-super nice to get him to keep talking. "We need to think bigger than that," she told him. "The best way to show that we're real scientists is to do some real science."

"Well, we could bring in my chickens," Theo said.

"But then we'll have to bring in live animals," Parker reminded him. "And that won't really show off our science skills."

Theo frowned. "But you want to bring in your guinea pig," he said. "He's a live animal too."

Even Cassie had her doubts. "What's the difference if we bring in one live animal or another?" she asked. "We might still get in trouble."

This was Parker's big moment. "We wouldn't have to bring Algebra to school," she told them. "We can make guinea pig robots instead."

"Guinea pig robots!" Theo said. His eyes were wider than Parker thought eyes could go. It was hard to tell, though, if that meant he was excited or peeved.

"How many would we have to make?" Cassie asked, opening her notebook. Parker knew she could count on Cassie to be practical.

Now Parker had to be practical too. She had to really think this through. For their presentation, they had to build robots that would show off guinea pig adaptations. So she thought about the ways guinea pigs had evolved in order to survive in the wild.

"We'll need one that squeaks," Parker said. "Because wild guinea pigs can make noises to alert their friends or ask for help."

Cassie wrote this trait down in her notebook, then looked up. "Algebra can run pretty fast for such a little guy," she said. "Would that help him escape predators?"

"Yes!" Parker loved this.

"I read once that guinea pigs can eat their own poop to get extra nutrients," Theo said.

"Well, Algebra doesn't do that, but maybe some guinea pigs do," Parker said. "Let's look it up. Maybe we could make a robot that eats little pellets. So instead of pooping everywhere like a live animal would, it would *eat* poop."

Here they were, her best friend in the world and someone who was maybe-kind-of-sort-of becoming a friend, all thinking like scientists!

Her maybe-kind-of-sort-of friend nodded as if he was thinking it all over.

Theo might not have been much good at science in second grade, but he was clearly a scientist in the making now. Plus, he was talking more and more. It seemed like science and Parker being extra-super nice were making him more chatty. She would have to record this evidence to help her draw conclusions about her Theo experiment. Later. After they'd proved themselves to be top-notch, award-winning scientists.

"I think we should also have lots of baby guinea pigs to show how fast they multiply!" Parker said. "It helps keep the species from any danger of going extinct."

For a minute, the only sound in the Mad Science Lab was the scribbling of Cassie's pencil as she jotted down ideas. Theo scratched his chin. Parker was so thrilled they were actually considering her plan!

Cassie looked at Parker. Parker looked at Theo. Theo gave them both a huge grin.

"Let's make robots!" he said. "How hard can it be?"

Parker Bell felt like it was finally her turn to feed Snodgrass and she was about to eat a cricket. She was ready to plan and design and build. And her two friends were by her side to do it.

Chapter 11

An Army of Rodents

The problem was that having an idea and putting it into action were two very different things.

"If we're going to make one squeak, could we make it talk, too?" Cassie asked. "Then it could tell the audience cool guinea pig facts."

"But we're supposed to show actual animal adaptations," Parker argued. "And guinea pigs are awesome, but they definitely don't speak human."

"I'm still not sure how we're going to make it squeak at all," Theo added, not at all helpfully.

All they had done was talk in circles about what they could do, without actually deciding how to do any of it.

"This is harder than I thought it would be," Cassie said.

It's one thing to make a generic robot — any scientist or engineer could do that. It was another thing entirely to make a whole bunch of bots that acted like guinea pigs.

There were so many factors to consider. Should they use solar panels or batteries? Have legs or wheels? Add fur or not? How would they make the eyes? And how could they get a robot guinea pig to squeak good and loud?

Parker's dad knocked at the door of the lab. He had three glasses of milk for them and some of his world-famous chocolate chip cookies.

"How's it going up here?" her dad asked. "Usually it's a lot noisier when you're at work."

"That's because we're not really at work yet," Parker told him.

"We need a plan before we can start," Cassie added. "You know how important a plan is."

"I do," Parker's dad said. "You have to figure out at least a basic recipe before you can start trying to make the perfect brownie."

"Yes!" Parker said. Her dad always understood. "You need a basic plan before you can build a robot, too."

Her dad popped a cookie into his mouth. "Sometimes it's good to start with what you already have in the kitchen," he said, heading for the stairs. "Then you can build a more complicated recipe from there."

Parker, Cassie, and Theo nibbled on their cookies and thought hard.

"Maybe we should just start building the first robot like I did in the trivia game," Cassie said. "First its head, then its body. Like Ultra-Megabot."

The skin on Parker's nose began to twitch. She felt like she had been shooting down all of Cassie's ideas, and that wasn't good teamwork. So how was she supposed to tell her BFF that you couldn't actually build a robot that way? She hoped Theo would say something before Parker had to. He seemed like he also knew a bit about robots.

But Theo kept eating his cookie and didn't say a

word. It figured he had to pick that moment to stop talking again. It was all going to be up to Parker.

"The thing is," Parker said, "you can't really build a robot that way."

"I did in the game!" Cassie replied.

"I know, but a game is just a simulation," Parker said. "You have to try to build one in real life to make sure your simulation works." She paused and took a deep breath. "And I've made lots of robots. You can't do it that way."

"Then how can you do it?" came a Theo-size voice from behind his cookie.

It was the perfect question. This was how science was supposed to work! By asking questions and trying to find answers, even if they weren't the ones you were looking for when you started.

"First you have to put a motor together," Parker said. "And figure out what kind of power the robot is going to use to run."

"Like plugging it into the wall or something?" Cassie asked.

"Exactly!" Parker said. "Except we wouldn't be able to plug these in during the assembly. So we'd need batteries or another power source."

"Cool!" Cassie said. "Can we use solar panels?"

"It would be tricky," Parker said. "We'd need to find a way to use the panels to precharge a battery since there's not enough sunlight in the auditorium, but we could probably do it."

"Fierce!" Cassie said. "Then what?"

"Then we need to connect all the robot's moving parts to the power source."

"Like wheels?" Theo offered.

"And the squeaking sounds!" Cassie added.

"And a jaw that opens and closes to eat poop," Parker said. "Which will be gross *and* fierce robotics all at the same time."

"So where do we get all this stuff?" Cassie said.

That was an easy question. "I have a lot of it here, actually," Parker said.

Together, they started digging through the Mad Science Lab. Theo found a wheel carriage in a

robotic bug kit that they could use for the running robot. Cassie found a model of a shark Parker had built two years ago with a jaw that could open and close. Now they just had to figure out how to make a robot squeak.

Parker went through a few robot kits and bins of parts but couldn't find anything that would work. Then she looked at Ultra-Megabot. The long-lasting LED light bulb went off in her head. She had a great idea, but it wasn't going to be easy to do.

Parker picked up the Ultra-Megabot robot she'd built herself and started sifting through her tools.

"What are you doing?" Cassie asked her.

"Ultra-Megabot has a voice recorder in him," Parker replied. "You can play his voice or up to five others."

"Cool!" Cassie said.

"Fierce!" Parker agreed. "I've never used the voice recorder. I always liked using his real voice. So I'm going to take him apart and use the recorder for the guinea pig squeaks."

Theo's jaw dropped. "You're going to destroy Ultra-Megabot?"

"We need his parts," Parker said.

Even though it meant taking apart a robot Parker had spent two months putting together, Cassie had been right: sometimes you had to sacrifice for science. Parker realized that now. Just as the cricket she planned to eat would realize it when it was her turn to feed Snodgrass.

Carefully, Theo and Cassie took the pieces from the kits and laid them out on a worktable. There were wheels, legs, gears, and control panels with energy inputs, power buttons, and microcontrollers everywhere. Then the two helped Parker take Ultra-Megabot apart. They did it in surprisingly little time, considering how long it had taken Parker to put him together.

For the robots' bodies, they used plastic Slinkys to make fake ribs. The three friends jerry-rigged solar panels so that the panels connected through each robot's control board to rechargeable batteries.

That way the robots could be put out in the sun to get the batteries good and ready, but they wouldn't need direct sunlight to make them run. The team decided not to use remote controls so the robots would move entirely on their own and seem more like real guinea pigs.

Parker's mom popped into the Mad Science Lab. "Do you three scientists at work need me to pick up any supplies for you?"

"We'll definitely need some furry material from the fabric store to cover the robots," Parker said.

"And some shiny buttons for eyes too, please!" Cassie added.

"Done!" Parker's mom said with a smile.

Sure, her mom might not be like her in any way, but she still really understood Parker's love of science sometimes. Especially when that love of science didn't mean taking apart the toaster. Or the emergency radio with the crank. Or the hand-held mini-vacuum.

Okay, so Parker had taken apart a lot of appliances. But when she wasn't doing that, her mom was totally into Parker's experiments.

○ ○ ○

It took them hours to build most of the robots, and Parker's mom had to go to three different stores to get all the materials they ended up needing. By the time her friends left, there was only one last robot that still needed to be finished, and Parker had to do this part on her own. She took Algebra out of his cage and put the voice recorder down next to him. She had to fiddle with the device to figure out how to make it record, but after some trial and error, she got it working.

"Okay, sweet furry boy, now's your chance to be a scientific star!" she told him.

At first Algebra didn't make a peep. Then he started to purr when she petted him under the chin.

Sound number one: recorded! But how was she going to get him to squeak nice and loudly when he seemed like he was in a quiet mood?

Parker thought it over. If guinea pigs' wild cousins squeaked to communicate with one another, maybe this guinea pig in her house would do the same if he saw another guinea pig. She carried Algebra and the recording device across the room and held her little piggy up to her mirror.

Algebra looked. Algebra sniffed. Then he sniffed again.

Finally, he started squeaking. At first it was soft little tweeting noises: voice recording number two! But soon enough he got going for real with some good, loud squeakiness.

Voice recording number three was done. Those three sounds were all they really needed to show how guinea pigs communicated. So, okay, one of the recordings started to play when it wasn't supposed to. But after Parker hit play and stop multiple times with no problems, it seemed like this little bug had worked itself out. She was sure that wouldn't happen again during their presentation.

She snuggled Algebra close to her. "I knew you'd be a great lab assistant," she said, smooching his head.

The fact was, between recording Algebra and all the hard work her team had done, Parker was in mad science heaven. She just knew that she was going to follow in the footsteps of Jane and Mae and win the gold medal for science!

Chapter 12

Bad Scientist at Work

It was finally the day of the Animal Adaptation Presentations and Parker was running late. Not horribly late, but still pretty late. No matter what her mom thought, it was hard work picking just the right outfit for such a big day.

Her dad knocked at her bedroom door.

"Time to get dressed!" he said. "Mom's holding the fort in the bakery so I can make you a special breakfast. But she has to leave for school soon."

If there was one thing that could get Parker moving quickly, it was her dad's cooking. She could already smell bacon from down the hall.

"Okay, I'll be right there!" she told him. Then she turned to her closet.

Parker already knew that you had to look your best to feel your best. Since her theory about dressing like a fierce animal to show her fierce interest in science had yielded good results before, Parker felt she could rely on it again. She put on her best leopard print dress with black leggings and black ballerina flats. A leopard headband completed the outfit.

"You look fierce," her dad said as she walked into the kitchen.

"Thanks, Dad!" Parker said with her hugest smile.

Her dad had always understood her fashion sense. Not that he dressed fancy himself. He usually wore jeans and was covered in flour. Her mom was even worse. Sure, she had to wear sweatpants to work as a PE teacher, but she did *not* have to wear them at home. She just liked to. Parker tried hard to respect her parents' personal styles of dressing, but it wasn't always easy.

She could always appreciate her dad's personal style of cooking, though: scrambled eggs, bacon, and a little cup of fresh fruit with yogurt on top.

"I figured you could use some protein," her dad said. "For the big day."

"Well, if you want to be like a leopard, you have to eat like one," Parker agreed. Today, she was going to be as strong as a leopard. *And* she was going to show the whole school that she could understand what made animals tick, like Jane Goodall did with chimpanzees, and be a scientific trailblazer, like Mae Jemison was when she became the first African American woman in space. To make it even better, Parker was going to have her best friend and her slowly-getting-to-be-good friend right there with her!

o o o

For such a big day, it sure did drag by. The presentations weren't until the afternoon and the wait was endless. Parker wished she was better at waiting.

She tried to observe Snodgrass in his tank. She tried to focus on what it would feel like to have a live, moving cricket in her mouth. Normally this would have made the waiting easier. But this presentation was much bigger than the Big Science Announcement. The whole Triathlon was on the line.

None of her usual tricks were working. All she could think about was how it felt like the Animal Adaptation Presentations were never going to start.

Somehow, suddenly, her lunch was in her stomach, recess was over, and Triathlon teams were getting ready in the auditorium. Parents and grandparents started to arrive. The other classes in her school sat on the floor in front of the presentation area Ms. Garcia had set up.

Parker's parents filed into the room and squeezed into chairs next to Cassie's parents and Theo's dad.

"Is your mom coming too?" Parker whispered to Theo.

Parker kept thinking she'd seen Theo get as red as you could get without being a tomato frog. But he kept managing to get redder. She had maybe started to figure out how to get Theo to talk more, but she wished she could also figure out a way to help him feel less red and worried all the time.

Theo took a deep breath. "My mom lives in Chicago now," he said in a voice even quieter than Parker's. "That's why I started taking the bus. Dad doesn't have time to drop me here and get to work in the morning."

Parker had not been expecting that at all. She wondered if his mom moving was part of the reason why he looked so anxious all the time.

"Are they divorced?" Cassie asked.

"Not yet." Theo's eyes dropped down to the floor. He looked so sad.

Parker knew she had to do something to make him feel better. This wasn't about proving her hypothesis and predictions anymore. It was about being a good friend. She had an idea. She almost couldn't believe she was about to say it out loud.

"Would you want to build a contraption to feed

your chickens together sometime?" she asked him. "I built one for Algebra and it's amazing."

She'd actually just offered to spend more time with Theo. The weird thing was, she wasn't dreading it. Sure, she had started the experiment with him mostly so he wouldn't steal Cassie from her. But Theo was all right. And she really did want to be his friend now.

Just as Theo opened his mouth to reply, Aidan, Braidan, and Jaidan's mom walked into the auditorium holding a live chicken in a cage. Aidan was next to her, holding a tiny chick and a dozen eggs in a carton under his arm.

"The Dempseys are doing *chickens?*" Cassie said.

"Why does everyone love chickens so much?" Parker asked.

This time Theo didn't turn red. He turned a little bit green. At that moment, he looked surprised and a little bit worried, like her mom had when she found the bacteria Parker had grown in her Mad Science Lab using gunk from inside her own nose.

"But we have robots," Parker reassured him. "Fierce guinea pig robots."

That sounded bonkers even to her. If there was one thing guinea pigs weren't, it was fierce.

Cassie raised a doubtful eyebrow, but Theo came in for the save. "Squeaking, running, poop-eating guinea pig robots with hordes of babies," he said.

"Which clearly show their adaptations while also showing off our amazing engineering skills," Parker added with a huge smile.

With a shake of her head, Cassie said, "I guess you're right. But that chick looks super cute and fuzzy."

Ms. Garcia called the classes to order. It was time for the Animal Adaptation Presentations!

First, there was one on monarch butterflies. The

girls from Mr. Tanner's class had made a model of a monarch eating from a milkweed plant.

"That looks beautiful!" Parker said under her breath.

The monarch team did a fierce presentation with lots of cool information. There wasn't a boring poster in sight. They clearly had done some hard work.

Next up was a presentation on porcupines and then one on snakes and how they shed their skins and open their jaws. There was another presentation on fish that live in deadly coral in tropical seas. That team had brought in a whole fish tank. Parker felt terrible that she'd made such a fuss about bringing in live animals. But live animals sitting in tanks and cages still weren't real science or engineering.

Then the Dempsey Triplets and their chickens were up.

Jaidan and Braidan were being surprisingly quiet and well-behaved, though they didn't add much to the presentation. Aidan did all the talking, and he carefully explained how hard an egg's shell was, how the mother hen's dense feathers kept her and her eggs warm, and how the down of the chick insulated it after it cracked out of its egg.

He said all the things Theo probably would have said for a chicken presentation.

He also had a papier-mâché model of a chick's shell to show how it was harder in some places than others and how a chick got out when it was ready to hatch.

Aidan had given a totally fierce and totally scientific presentation. Parker was about to tell him just that when Ms. Garcia called her team up.

Their presentation was last, and Parker was ready. She stood up straight and tall and turned on the first two guinea pig robots. Cassie talked about all the babies they can have, and how guinea pigs can run fast to escape predators, as Theo set up the eater robot. The other kids at Eleanor Roosevelt Elementary *loved* the poop-eating guinea pig. Theo even used a good, loud voice to tell the audience about the

nutrients the piggies gained from doing something so gross.

Their team was slaying its Animal Adaptation Presentation!

Then Parker turned on the squeaking guinea pig robot and began to explain how they used noises to communicate. She tried to turn from the purr (noise number one) to the soft tweeting sounds (noise number two), but all she got was a big earful of noise number three: Algebra's loudest, most in-your-face squeaks.

And she couldn't turn them back off again.

Cassie and Theo tried to help, but the switch not only stopped working, it broke off! Maybe the recording device was too old and didn't work properly anymore? Maybe Parker hadn't hooked it up right? Guinea pig squeaking filled the auditorium. It wouldn't have been too bad, except the noise set the hen to squawking as well. Even the little chick got in on the noise-making action.

Soon the whole auditorium was filled with

robotic and real animals making a lot of loud noises. Everyone looked startled by the racket, even the fish in the tank. Just when she thought it couldn't get any worse, Parker knocked the pellet-eating robot off the presentation stand and it made a beeline for the kindergartners sitting on the floor in the front. The jaw of the robot opened and closed. The little kids screamed and scrambled to get away.

It was complete chaos.

For the first time in her life, Parker didn't feel like a mad scientist. She felt like a *bad* scientist. And it wasn't a very good feeling.

Chapter 13

(Not So) Gold Medal Science

Parker made a dive for the pellet-eating guinea pig and hit the off switch. The kindergartners stopped screaming, but then they started doing something even worse: giggling. The robot and chicken noises were joined by the horrible laughing sounds of first the little kids, then the whole school.

"What are we going to do?" Cassie asked.

"Did you bring any tools to remove the batteries?" Theo asked.

With a sad shake of the head, Parker said, "No, I didn't think of it."

They handed the squeaking robot around, each trying to do something (anything!) to stop the noise, but nothing worked. The guinea pig kept squeaking, and the hen seemed to think the robot was talking to her, so she kept clucking right back.

Parker wasn't going to be an award-winning scientist like Jane and Mae. Instead, she had built a robot that didn't work. And she'd let her friends down at the same time. In the end, Mr. Jones in maintenance had to come and give them screwdrivers and pliers to take the talking guinea pig apart. With a sad whirring sound, the squeaking finally stopped. On the other side of the auditorium, Parker could see Aidan, and even Braidan and Jaidan, comforting their chicken and little chick. They were all being really sweet and gentle with the birds.

The only sounds left in the auditorium at Eleanor Roosevelt Elementary School were the last snickers of their fellow students, who'd thought the whole thing had been very, very funny.

Finally, Ms. Garcia cleared her throat at the front of the auditorium and raised her three fingers, the school signal for silence. Everyone, even the kindergartners, went quiet.

"Well, those were certainly more eventful Animal Adaptation Presentations than I thought they would be," she said.

Parents chuckled at the back of the room. *Everyone* was laughing at Parker and Cassie and Theo.

"Our Triathlon students did so much hard work over the past few weeks," Ms. Garcia continued, "with their Animal Adaptation Presentations today, and also the Science Bee and their Egg Drop designs."

The crowd politely clapped, but Parker knew they weren't really clapping for her team. Parker, Cassie, and Theo had done so well in the Science Bee, but everything had been a mess with the Egg Drop. They had needed this presentation to win the Triathlon, and instead they had blown it. And it wasn't like her whole team had blown it together: Parker had blown it for them by insisting they make guinea pig robots and then by making a squeaking one that didn't work right.

"Principal Warren has made her final decision about the awards, so let's announce them and get this finished up," Ms. Garcia said. "I mean, let's celebrate everybody's efforts in the name of science!"

Principal Warren came to the front of the room with three sets of medals: gold, silver, and bronze. This was it. The big moment Parker had been waiting three long weeks for.

"In third place," Principal Warren said, "for artistic work and scientific knowledge, are Aidan, Jaidan, and Braidan Dempsey!"

Jaidan and Braidan were busy snuggling their chicken, so Aidan went up to get their medals. This seemed only fair since he was the one who'd done all the work anyway.

Parker smiled at him as he sat down again. "Good job," she mouthed to him. Aidan grinned at her.

"And in second place," Principal Warren continued, "for scientific ingenuity and some very ambitious robotics, we have Parker Bell, Cassie Malouf, and Theo Zachary!"

Parker couldn't believe they got second place. Second wasn't bad, of course. But her team probably would have won gold if it wasn't for her.

Cassie nudged her. "Come on, let's get our medals!" she said.

Parker got up slowly from her seat and accepted her silver medal. She was relieved that they'd still gotten medals, but second place wasn't the achievement she had imagined when she signed up for the Triathlon. She wasn't sure what she was feeling anymore. Disappointed they didn't win gold? Afraid her friends would be mad at her for messing up their presentation? Even a little admiration for Aidan, who seemed to have gotten a bronze medal without any help at all from his fellow triplets?

In the end, the monarch butterfly girls from Mr. Tanner's class won first place. Parker couldn't really argue with the choice. They'd done a lot of research and made an amazing display, and they had done a great job on the other events. What had Parker made? A mess of everything.

Parker slumped into her chair. While Cassie usually never got mad at Parker, this might be the one time she did. And Parker was sure Theo was mad at her too. After all, she was the one who'd shot down the ideas for both monarchs *and* chickens. Parker thought back to second grade when she and Theo had been science partners. Sure, Theo had wrecked their sink-or-float experiment. But Parker had wrecked the entire Science Triathlon, which was a *much* bigger deal.

The Science Triathlon, like her friendship experiment, had not yielded the results she'd thought it would.

Chapter 14

Always a Silver Lining

Cassie's family and Theo's dad agreed to come back to the bakery for a postpresentation treat. When she got there, Parker went upstairs to change. The leopard-print dress that she had been so happy to wear that morning went straight into the laundry. There was no use dressing like a fierce animal if you weren't going to act like one.

The green skirt and top she changed into made her look more like a plant than an animal, and her sneakers were the most boring shoes ever.

Parker was feeling very *blah*.

When she went downstairs, the sound of talking and laughing hit her ears. Theo's dad was chatting with Cassie's parents and Parker's mom. Theo and Cassie had the poop-eating and running robotic guinea pigs out on the table where they were sitting. Parker was surprised to see the Dempsey Triplets sitting in a corner of the bakery with their dad.

Parker's own dad was putting out a tray full of cookies he'd set aside for them earlier in the day. "To celebrate your great work in the Science Triathlon," he told her.

Parker wasn't sure what there was to celebrate.

She went to sit with Cassie and Theo and picked at her chocolate chip cookie. She was too anxious to enjoy it the way she usually did. She felt like the old mouse bones in the owl poop she'd dissected last summer at science camp: dried up, cracked up, and just plain bad.

"What's wrong?" Theo asked. "I thought you'd be happy that we won second place."

"She wanted a gold medal in science," Cassie explained. "So she could be like Jane Goodall and Mae Jemison."

Parker took a deep breath. "I did," she admitted.

"But silver's okay too." Then she looked at her friends. "At least, it would be if I hadn't made us lose the gold."

Theo and Cassie gave each other strange looks.

"How did you make us lose the gold?" Cassie asked.

"The squeaking robot!" Parker said. "If I hadn't messed up the voice recorder, we would have won."

"I don't know," Cassie said. "Our project was still way scientific."

"And if we'd only made a poster for one of our other ideas, we might not have won anything," Theo added.

"Plus, good science doesn't always go the way you think it's going to," Cassie put in.

Parker took a minute to let that sink in. Jane Goodall hadn't started off being a world-famous chimpanzee expert after all, had she? It had taken lots of time observing and trying out strategies on how to work with the animals so that they trusted her. And it had taken Mae Jemison years to become a doctor, not to mention all the hard work she'd had to do to become an astronaut.

Even if her team hadn't won the Science Triathlon, Parker could still work toward being the very best scientist she could be.

After all, her experiment with Theo hadn't exactly gotten the results she'd anticipated. Sure, he was talking more. And he wasn't trying to steal Cassie from her. But Parker still wasn't sure if he wanted to be *her* friend.

"So you're not mad at me?" Parker asked.

Theo let out a little laugh. "No," he said. "I thought maybe you were mad at me, though."

"Because of the presentation?" Parker asked. "Why would I be mad about that? I'm the one who messed up."

"No, about the sink-or-float experiment in second grade," he told her. "You've kind of seemed mad at me ever since that day."

Parker wasn't sure what to say. She had definitely

been mad at the time, but not anymore. Not for ages. Suddenly, Theo not talking to her was making a lot more sense.

"No way," she told Theo. "I'm not mad at you at all. And I'm . . . I'm glad we were a team for the Triathlon."

"And made the best guinea pig robots ever," Theo said.

"Plus, I thought we slayed the Animal Adaptation Presentation," Cassie added. "The squeaking was amazing."

Just as Parker was back to feeling like her usual great self again, someone tapped her shoulder. She slumped in her chair. The only person who ever poked at her was Jaidan, and she *really* hoped he wasn't coming to tease her.

She turned to tell Jaidan to bug off, but Aidan was standing there instead.

"Your robots were fierce," he said. "Were they hard to build?"

"Yes!" Parker and Cassie and Theo all said at the same time.

"I've never built a robot before," Aidan said. He looked down at the floor and turned a little bit red, just like Theo used to.

"Maybe you could help us with the next one we build?" Parker said to him.

Aidan turned even redder, but he smiled, too.

Parker was up for the idea. If Aidan could turn out to be a top-rate scientist, he might be a top-rate friend, too. Theo had, and Parker hadn't expected that at all!

Then, out of nowhere, Ms. Garcia came to their table. She was carrying a coffee cup and a to-go bag of bakery treats.

"Nice job with the chickens and the robot rodents," she told the group. "Even if things got a little out of control for a while."

Sure, Parker's friends weren't angry at her . . . but maybe Ms. Garcia was? It was as if a dark cumulonimbus cloud had come to hail all over Parker's day again.

"Seeing as you three are so good at building robots, I was wondering if you'd want to start a robotics club," Ms. Garcia said.

Suddenly the cumulonimbus cleared.

"A robotics club?" Parker repeated.

"Yes — you could put up flyers," Ms. Garcia said. "And meet in our classroom after school to help other students learn to build robots. Does that sound good?"

Parker wasn't in any clubs, but she wanted to be.

"Amazing!" Parker said.

"Extra-super great!" Cassie said.

"Fierce!" Theo added.

"I'll be your first member," Aidan said as he walked back to his brothers.

Parker and Cassie and Theo all grinned.

They were going to have their very own robotics club at school! Plus, Parker was going to get to run it

with her two friends. And Aidan would be in it too. This was going to be the best thing ever.

Parker held out one hand to Cassie. She held the other out to Theo. For the first time ever, Theo locked knuckles with her. They danced their fingers around and burst out laughing.

All in one day, Parker had become an award-winning scientist (a silver medal was still an award!), got to start a robotics club, and was now maybe-kind-of-sort-of friends with Aidan *and* BFFs with Theo and Cassie. Maybe she could finally explain to Theo that he'd stolen her and Cassie's seat on the bus? Or maybe it didn't matter that much if she and Cassie sat in the fifth seat on the left. Or maybe she could make a chart so they could all take turns sitting in the sixth seat on the left.

Parker loved making charts.

She already had plans swirling in her head for their new club.

Parker sat with her friends thinking about robots and cookies. She was going to wear her silver medal and eat as many chocolate chip cookies as she possibly could. Cookies today, crickets tomorrow. Or in a few weeks when she launched a whole new experiment on eating bugs. Because Parker had big scientific plans, and her fellow mad scientists to help her put those plans into action.